D0595569

Stars of Wonder:
A Children's Christmas Adventure

Written by Rebecca Dwight Bruff
Illustrated by Jill Dubin

Published by

An imprint of

3705 Shore Drive
Virginia Beach, VA 23455
800-435-4811
www.koehlerbooks.com

STARS
of
Wonder

A Children's Christmas Adventure

Written By

REBECCA DWIGHT BRUFF

Illustrated By

JILL DUBIN

The author has noticed that, by strange and rare coincidence, the characters in this story share the names of real-life people who are indeed fine and brave, and include a princess and three fine princes.

They are, truly, stars of wonder.

*T*ell us again, Nana, about the magic people that went to see the new king!

The magic people? Whoever are you talking about?

You remember! The magics from far away. They rode on camels.

Magics?

Yes! They were really smart, and they saw a ginormous star and they knew a new king was there where the star was going, so they followed the big star.

*Oh, the magi! They weren't magic exactly, but they were called magi. They were smart, that's right. Sometimes people called them the **Wise Men**. They were probably royal, like princes.*

Just princes? Are you serious? Why wasn't there a princess?

Oh, of course there was a princess! There's always a princess in great stories of royalty and wisdom and bravery and love.

Tell us again, Nana. I think Jay-bug was too little last time, and he doesn't remember.

CHAPTER 1

A VERY LONG TIME AGO, in a place far away, there lived a royal family: three fine brothers, all princes, and their lovely sister, the princess.

They lived in a beautiful village near the ocean, and played on white-sand beaches and took naps under swaying palm trees.

And at night, under the stars, their mother and father taught them all about the moon and the sun and the stars, even the constellations.

One night as they lay on their blankets looking up into the heavens, Princess Phoebe thought she saw a new star.

"Mama!" she whispered. They whispered at night because the soft winds and the calls of the owls and the sound of the waves created such beautiful music.

"Mama, look! That star! I think it's new. I don't remember seeing it before."

The oldest brother, Prince Jonah, had noticed the star too, and he was proud of his sister for seeing it, and for asking about it, because he also wondered if it was new.

The youngest brother, Prince Jacob, forgot to whisper. "It's the youngest, newest star, but it's so bright!" he said excitedly.

The middle brother, Prince Nathan, had been watching the star very carefully. "That is a special star," he said quietly, with a voice full of awe and wonder.

Night after night the family watched the bright new star, and every night it grew a little brighter.

It seemed to be moving from east to west across the vast night sky.

The princes and the princess were eager students, and they loved math and art and geography and history and literature and science because they knew the world wanted to teach them so much. They *also* liked to play **kick-and-run**. It was a game they invented, which centuries later became known as **soccer.**

So, one morning after they finished their lessons and playing, they sat down for a snack and overheard their mother and father talking.

"It's extraordinary!" they heard Royal Mama say.

"Indeed it is! It's never happened before and may never happen again, and we get to witness it in our own night sky," Royal Papa agreed.

What could this extraordinary thing be? the royal and wise children wondered as they kept listening.

"I think— No, I *believe*," their father was saying, "that this fine bright star is leading the way to a new king, the greatest king the world has ever known!"

"But where?" asked Royal Mama. "Where is this fine new king to be found?"

"Ah, that is the question, my love," said Royal Papa. "I suppose we'll never know, for he is surely far, far away. A person would have to follow the star, wherever it leads. It could be a journey of many days, maybe longer. I'm afraid we shall never know."

That afternoon, after swimming in the clear blue ocean waters, the princess and her princely brothers sat on the warm sand. They all seemed to have the same idea.

"We should follow the star and find the great king," said Prince Nathan.

"It would be a wonderful adventure," said Prince Jonah, "but we would have to be brave because it might be dangerous."

"Well, we *are* brave," said Princess Phoebe.

Prince Jacob jumped to his feet. "When do we start? I'm ready!"

Prince Jonah began writing in the sand with his finger. He was making a list.

"Here's what we need," he said, pointing to what he had written:

Our camels
Our snacks
Our water
Our blankets

"Am I forgetting anything?" he asked his royal siblings. They were quiet.

Prince Nathan said, "Perhaps we should take a gift to the king."

"Yes!" Princess Phoebe agreed. "And cake! With sprinkles!"

Prince Jacob added, "And a ball to kick!"

Prince Jonah nodded. "And some books to read!"

Prince Nathan suggested, "Something from here to show how we journeyed so far . . . I know! We'll take our special frankincense!"

"Yes!" They agreed that all of their ideas were perfect.

"But," said Prince Jonah, "there's one little issue."

"What?" they all asked together.

"We don't know very much about taking care of the camels on such a long journey. I think we should ask Sumar to come with us. He's a good friend, and trustworthy. And knows *everything* about camels."

They all agreed. Their good friend Sumar, son of the village camel breeder, would join them. He, too, was strong and brave and smart. And he did, in fact, know everything about camels.

The royal brothers and sister agreed that they wouldn't mention their plans to their parents, because they didn't want them to worry. This was not their best idea, they realized in retrospect.

★ ★ ★

A few days later, in the middle of the night, when no one else in the entire village was awake, the very quiet caravan left the village, following a bright, bright star. They formed a line:

First Jonah
    and Sumar,
        then Princess Phoebe,
            Prince Nathan,
                and Prince Jacob.

For three long days and nights, they rode, stopping only to eat a bit and rest the camels in a tiny spot of shade

under an occasional palm tree during the day. At night, they built a small fire and ate and rested, and every night the star shone bigger and brighter!

On the fourth day, they saw a great palace in the distance.

Who lives there? they all wondered.

"We'll find out tomorrow," said Prince Jonah. "Let's rest here tonight, and tomorrow we'll meet the ruler who lives in the grand palace."

★ ★ ★

That night, just as they spread their blankets under the sky where the big star seemed even brighter, the camels began to growl and snort and stomp, as if in warning.

Something was wrong!

And suddenly, appearing at the crest of a big sand dune, they saw a pair of golden eyes glowing in the dark. And then another pair. And then another.

Three hungry mountain lions had smelled their dinner from the hills in the distance.

The princess and Sumar and the three princely brothers all jumped to their feet, filled with both fear and courage, because it is true that **fear** and **courage** often happen together.

They each grabbed a big long stick from the pile of wood next to their fire.

"Protect the camels!" shouted Sumar as he ran between the hungry lions and the frightened camels.

Just then, the biggest of the mountain lions leapt past Sumar and knocked a camel to the ground. Sumar swung at the mountain lion with all his might, and Princess Phoebe joined him.

At the same time, Prince Jacob and Prince Nathan and Prince Jonah fought against the other two lions, swinging their sticks and yelling, and they chased them back over the dune and watched them run toward the hills.

But when they turned around, they saw a terrible sight. Their father's best camel, Jasmine, was on the ground with horrible bloody gashes on her legs, and Princess Phoebe and Sumar, having chased the lion away, were both bleeding too. The lion's claws had ripped Princess Phoebe's right arm, and torn the flesh on Sumar's left leg.

But they were both laughing!

"Phoebe! Sumar! What happened? Are you okay?" Prince Jonah shouted as he ran to his sister.

Sumar and Princess Phoebe both smiled, even though they were hurt.

"We showed that lion a thing or two!" laughed Princess Phoebe. "Sumar whacked him good, and he limped when he ran away!"

"But you should have seen Princess Phoebe," said Sumar with a smile. "She is a fierce warrior! She clobbered that old cat, and her shouting almost scared *me* away!"

Prince Jonah and Prince Nathan and Prince Jacob were so proud of Princess Phoebe and Sumar. And the princess and Sumar were equally proud of the brave princely brothers.

But soon they recognized that they were in a bit of a pickle. Jasmine the Camel would need time to rest and heal before traveling again.

After cleaning and bandaging one arm, one leg, and one camel, the five brave adventurers talked for a long time, trying to decide what to do.

"If we stay here, we'll not be able to follow the star to the king," Prince Nathan said.

"But we can't go, not with Jasmine the Camel so wounded, and the princess and Sumar both need to rest as well," Prince Jacob said.

"We must think," said Prince Jonah.

And they all thought hard.

After a long silence beneath the bright star, Princess Phoebe offered an idea.

"I think Sumar and I should stay here with Jasmine

the Camel, while the three of you journey on. You'll arrive at the big palace tomorrow, and perhaps they can tell you how far it is to the king. I think we must be close by now."

"Yes!" said Sumar. "You can visit the king and deliver our gifts and then return to us. The princess and Jasmine and I should be strong again by then, and we could all go together to the king or return to our home, whichever you learn is best."

"I don't know," said Prince Jonah. "Will you be okay?"

"Did you see how brave they were?" asked Prince Jacob.

"What do *you* think, brother Nathan?" asked the royal sister.

Prince Nathan thought hard. "I think our sister is right. We three princes should continue. We'll stay at the palace tomorrow and then go find the new king. We'll be back here in just a few more days."

Prince Nathan looked at his sister and Sumar. "You are both strong and brave. Sumar will take good care of Jasmine the Camel, but more importantly, you two will take good care of one another."

They all looked to Prince Jonah, because he was the oldest and they knew he was becoming a very wise man.

"Yes," Prince Jonah said quietly. "The star is leading us, and the new king is near, and we will all do our part. The three of us"—he pointed to his brothers—"will leave at sunrise. We will be back within a week."

It was agreed, and at sunrise the very next morning the three wise princes hugged the princess and Sumar, and got on their camels and headed westward across the sand toward the palace in the distance.

★ ★ ★

CHAPTER 2

Three days later, the princes had reached the palace of a grumpy man named Herod. While they were there dining, Princess Phoebe and Sumar were surprised by a visitor at their little campfire.

They had just checked on Jasmine the Camel, and warmed some soup on the fire to eat with their bread, when they heard a small voice.

"Can you help me?" the voice called. The sun was low on the horizon, and they looked up to see a little wrinkled old woman leaning on her walking stick.

"Hello," said Sumar. He wanted to be friendly and kind to the woman, but he was also watching to be sure there were no bandits hiding anywhere.

"You can't be too careful," he whispered to the princess. "Keep your eyes open!"

Sumar extended his hand to the old woman and looked at the twinkly eyes in her wrinkly face.

"Here," he said. "Let me help you." He led her to the campfire where the princess had folded some blankets to make a seat for her.

Princess Phoebe brought some cool water, and after she drank and drank, the old woman with the twinkly eyes said, "Thank you. I am Anna. You can call me Nana Anna."

"Why are you all alone in the desert, Nana Anna? And where are you going?" asked Princess Phoebe.

"Well, I don't know if you've noticed, but there's a bright new star in the sky, and I think it must lead to something or someone very special. I'm an old woman, but I'm not too old to follow a star."

Nana Anna was definitely old and very wise. She knew that star-following was important, no matter a person's age, or size, or personality, or where they were from, or what language they spoke, or what food they liked. This bright star in the sky was important to everyone.

Princess Phoebe and Sumar invited Nana Anna to stay with them for the night, before she followed the star again the next day. "We have plenty of food, and we have lots of water too, and Sumar and I are already digging a well . . . just in case!" said Princess Phoebe.

"Ah, how smart of you to think about **just in case**!" Nana Anna smiled. Her twinkly eyes were full of kindness.

Princess Phoebe and Sumar shared their food and water with Nana Anna, and then they put out the fire, and each one made a pillow from a camel blanket and fell asleep under the gentle stars.

★ ★ ★

While the three bold princes were with the grumpy King Herod, and while Princess Phoebe and Sumar were with Nana Anna, Royal Mama and Royal Papa were on camels in the very same desert, following the very same star and looking for them. Sumar's papa was with them, too, while Sumar's mama stayed in the village to watch for their children in case they came home.

Papa Sumar led them on his finest camel because he knew the sand dunes of the desert very well, and he knew how best to travel over them. He even knew where to find a small oasis with water.

"I am sure our adventurous children have come this way," he called to Royal Papa and Royal Mama behind him.

Mama smiled, in her **little-bit-worried** way. "I hope so," she whispered.

Papa laughed. "They are probably over the next sand dune!"

But, in truth, each of the grownups was a **little bit concerned**, because they loved their children very much and worried. They only wanted to find them, and to know that they were safe, and to hug them tight.

The sun slipped down the edge of the sky, and just as it disappeared behind a sand dune, the three worried grownups stopped at a quiet little oasis, and got off of their camels.

"We will need to stay here tonight," Papa Sumar said.

"What is this?" Royal Mama asked, holding up an apricot pit and the broken shells of some nuts. "I think I know where these came from!"

"They must be very near," said Royal Papa. "I'll go to the top of that dune and see if I see the light of a fire."

Royal Papa walked up and up and up to the top of the highest dune, and he looked as far as he could see in the desert moonlight. But he didn't see anything at all.

★ ★ ★

The next morning, two sand dunes away, Princess Phoebe noticed that Nana Anna wore a sparkly bracelet with five big, colorful beads.

Nana Anna noticed Princess Phoebe admiring the bracelet and the beads. *Ah*, she thought, *this princess is very observant, and she notices details. She's a very smart princess!*

Nana Anna asked, "Princess Phoebe, would you like to see my bracelet with its beads?"

"It's so pretty and interesting," said Princess Phoebe. "Is it very special to you?"

She thought it might be extra special because Nana Anna didn't seem to have many possessions.

"Oh, yes, it's as special as special can be! It reminds me of people I have loved and places and experiences that have filled my heart."

Princess Phoebe leaned in close to listen, and Nana Anna took the bracelet off of her wrist and held it in her hands.

She touched the first bead and said, "This bead is blue, like the sky and the water and the eyes of my **true love.** His name is Thomas."

Princess Phoebe thought Thomas must be quite kind and handsome and full of goodness.

Next, Nana Anna touched a golden bead. "This lovely bead is made of pure gold, and it reminds me that the sun comes up every day, no matter what, and that every new day is an invitation to open my heart to love and goodness."

Princess Phoebe thought that Nana Anna's heart, because it was so old, must be very full indeed.

A red bead, smooth and a little smaller than the others, was next. "This bead," said Nana Anna, "helps me remember that when I am angry or hurt, I'm not alone, and that I have enough strength inside of me and enough love around me to get through the hard and scary moments in life."

Princess Phoebe was quiet, wondering if Nana Anna had endured many hard and scary times.

Nana Anna spoke again, as if she knew what Princess Phoebe was thinking. "If you have a long life, like mine, you'll have some hard and scary days and some dark and lonely nights, and sometimes life will feel confusing and way too complicated, and you'll wonder if you can get through it." She paused, and was silent for a while. When she started speaking again, she spoke so quietly that Princess Phoebe had to listen very closely.

"You will get through it, and you will be stronger and wiser, but you must be careful that those frightening things don't let your heart get hard or cold. Remember that, my princess. Don't let your heart grow hard or cold, no matter what. Will you promise?"

"Yes, I promise." Phoebe nodded solemnly, wondering how a person protects her heart when it gets wounded.

"This bright-green bead reminds me that life is always a good gift, and that every living thing is sacred—green grass and green lizards and every living thing! When I think about **creation,** my heart grows stronger and warmer. Oh, Princess Phoebe, **life and love** are woven together, you know, and choosing a life with love is the most wondrous thing of all!"

Princess Phoebe smiled. She was young, yes, but she knew this must be true.

"What about this bead, Nana Anna?" She pointed to the fifth bead, so very pink that just looking at it made her smile.

"Oh, sweetheart, that is **joy,** the great gift of gladness because **life** is grand and **love** is real and **beauty** is everywhere. You must remember that, my dear!" Those words would live in a song many years in the future.

Princess Phoebe looked at the bracelet with its beads of blue and gold and red and green and very pink, trying to memorize the beautiful colors and their messages. She thought it might be the most important thing she had seen in all her life.

"May I give you this bracelet, Princess Phoebe?" asked Nana Anna.

"Give it to me? Oh, no, Nana Anna, no. I couldn't take something so special from you!"

"Oh, but you would be giving me a great gift if you would wear it, dear princess. You would not be taking it from me. You would be receiving something of great value. It has served me well, and I have learned its lessons, and they will always be with me."

They were both very quiet for a bit.

"May I give it to you, Princess?"

"I receive it with grateful love," Princess Phoebe said with deep respect and a lump in her throat. And with that, Nana Anna put the bracelet on Princess Phoebe's wrist, and they both knew a little bit more about **love** and **life.**

Meanwhile, Sumar was tending Jasmine the Camel, and he noticed that her wounds were healing so quickly you could almost call it a miracle.

At that exact same time, in the palace across the sands to the west, Prince Jonah and Prince Nathan and Prince Jacob were saying goodbye to the grumpy King Herod.

"Thank you for giving us a place to rest and such a nice meal. Now we can be on our way, to see where the bright star stops," said Prince Jonah. And the three bold princes mounted their camels and waved goodbye to the grumpy king and his queen and the servants of the palace.

"Don't forget to come back and tell me everything you see and learn," shouted the king as they rode away across the sand.

The three brave princes rode in silence all morning, thinking their own thoughts. As the sun fell hot on their shoulders in the middle of the day, Prince Nathan saw a cluster of palm trees and said, "Let's stop for a moment in the shade of the palms."

As they rested and cooled off in the shade, Prince Jacob said, "I have a funny feeling about the grumpy king."

"Me too," said Nathan. "He seemed a little *nefarious* to me."

"Why do you always have to use big words like that?" Prince Jacob asked. "What is a *na-fairy*?"

"He uses big words because they're just the right word!" exclaimed Prince Jonah. "You're right, Nathan. I couldn't quite put my finger on it, but he did seem nefarious. Exactly!"

"Will someone please tell me what that means?" Jacob insisted.

"It means he seems wicked," said Jacob.

"Evil," added Jonah.

"Villainous."

"Murderous."

"Vile."

"Atrocious."

"Foul."

"Diabolical."

"Okay, okay. I get it. A **bad guy**," said Prince Jacob. "Why didn't you just say so?"

"Yes, he seems like a bad guy," said Princes Jonah and Nathan in unison.

Prince Jonah added, "But we don't know if he's a bad guy. Maybe he's just grumpy and cranky. But I think we should be extra careful."

"What do you mean?" asked Prince Jacob.

"I don't know yet," answered Prince Jonah. "It's just a feeling I have."

The princes ate apricots and drank water and got back on their camels, even though the sun was still high and hot.

"It's not too far now," said Prince Nathan. "I think we can get there before dark!"

The star was so bright that they could see it even during the day. But they knew that the star was most beautiful and bright at night, and its movement had slowed. Maybe tonight it would find its final destination.

"I'm getting a little bored. We should sing a song," suggested Prince Jacob.

"What do you have in mind?" asked Prince Jonah. He knew that Jacob loved to sing, and hoped he would make a new song for their journey.

"We need a song about three princes traveling a long way to see a new king!" said Prince Nathan.

Prince Jacob thought hard, and then began singing:

We three princes are handsome, we are!
Now we're riding our camels so far.
The giant star leads us, the baby king needs us
To bring him the incense-filled jar.
Oh, oh! Star of wonder, star of might,
Star of royal beauty bright!

Suddenly, he stopped singing. "I don't know," he said. "That doesn't sound quite right. I'll try to think of something else."

"Look!" cried Prince Nathan, pointing to a tiny spot on the horizon. "In that little valley! Let's try to get there by sundown. It looks like there's a little barn where we could stay. It might be warmer than staying out here in the desert."

They urged their camels to move faster, and sure enough, just as the sun was setting, they arrived at the little barn.

"What is that sound?" asked Jacob.

"It sounds like a baby is crying," said Prince Nathan. "That's how you sounded when you were a baby!"

"I did not!" shouted Prince Jacob.

"Shhh!" Prince Jonah put his finger to his lips. "And look!" He pointed to the sky above them.

The star was **right there**. It was so bright and so beautiful that all three princes fell silent. For the rest of their lives, they would remember that night, and the brilliant star, and the warm, wondrous feeling of that moment—a feeling of holy wholeness.

The princes would learn that there are some moments so wondrous, and so extraordinary, and so beautiful that they live in one's heart forever. They remind one that **holiness and goodness** are true and real.

Without a sound, they slipped quietly off their camels and tiptoed into the barn. Inside was a lovely young woman holding a tiny baby. The baby had stopped crying, and the young woman with tired eyes smiled at the young man next to her, whose eyes were full of gentleness and wonder, and they both motioned for the three princes to come closer.

"How did you find us?" the young woman whispered.

"Who are you?" whispered Prince Jonah.

The man with the gentle eyes spoke very quietly. "This is Mary and I am Joseph, and this little one we call Jesus."

"He's so little," said Prince Jacob. "We thought he would be a grown-up king."

"Yes, he's little, but he's already very strong," laughed Mary. "He can make a big fuss when he's hungry or sleepy!"

"We brought him some gifts," said Prince Jonah. "Because the star is so special, we knew it would lead to someone extra special. But we didn't know it would be a teensy baby. These aren't really baby things."

"When he grows up, he'll understand," said Mary. "You're very kind. Where did you come from?"

"We started a few days ago, from *waaaaaay* over there," said Prince Nathan, pointing toward the eastern horizon. "We'll be going home soon."

"Last night we stayed at the fancy palace of the grumpy king," said Prince Jacob. "He told us to stop again on the way home to tell him what we've seen and learned from the star."

Joseph made a serious face.

"But we're not sure we should do that, even though he's the king and all. He seems a little nefarious," Prince Jacob continued. He was glad that he was able to use the big new word.

"Well," said Mary, "you definitely do not have to do what a nefarious person tells you to do. If you get that untrustworthy feeling about someone, you must trust your own feelings. They are called your **instincts**." Mary seemed wise beyond her years.

"What else did the grumpy king say?" asked Joseph.

Prince Jonah, because he was oldest, spoke on behalf of his royal brothers. "He seemed a little nervous, actually. When we told him we were on our way to meet a new king, he made a very angry face, and he got up from the table and stomped around. Then he sat back down and smiled, but it was a fake kind of smile."

Prince Jonah knew that often, when people are afraid or angry, they pretend to be just fine, or even happy.

Prince Nathan added, "He wanted to know a lot of details about the new king, but when we told him we didn't know anything, he huffed, and then put on his pretendy smile again."

"That's when he said, 'Well then, why don't you boys just come back and tell me everything after you meet the king?'" added Prince Jacob. "He said, 'Then I can go see him for myself.'"

"*Hmmm*," said Joseph. "That's not good. I think he must be feeling a bit threatened. Sometimes, kings like to be **the only important one**, and they never like the idea of another king. That's why they fight with each other so much."

Mary looked concerned. "This could be dangerous for our little one," she said quietly.

"We must think very carefully," said Prince Jonah.

"We must listen to our hearts," said Prince Nathan.

"We must be wise and brave," said Prince Jacob.

In that moment they each hoped that they were smart and wholehearted and wise and brave, and that they would make **good decisions** even when life was hard and confusing and complicated and scary.

Just then the sleeping baby woke up and smiled at the three princes, and in his smile they saw **perfect love**. The princes immediately knew that **perfect love** casts away all fear.

Jonah said, "Here's what I think. We should not go back to see the grumpy king. I think we should go back by a different way."

"Yes," Prince Nathan said. "My heart tells me we should protect the child and keep the **insecure one** from hurting him. We must take another path."

"I agree!" sang Jacob. "Grumpy King Nefariousness thinks he can be the boss of us. But he's wrong! This tiny **king of love** must live and grow. We will trick the bad king, and choose a better way!"

And so it was agreed. The three fine princes stayed with Mary and Joseph and the smiling baby all through the night, and they slept soundly. And as the sun rose the next morning, they said their goodbyes, kneeling at

the makeshift crib of the tiny King Jesus, and thanking him for shining his love on them.

The young princes knew **good and perfect love** when they saw it, and their hearts filled with wonder and gratitude. They couldn't help saying **thank you,** because they knew they would carry that **good and perfect love** in their hearts forever.

★ ★ ★

Meanwhile, back at the oasis, Princess Phoebe and Sumar said goodbye to Nana Anna as she set out to follow the star saying, "I just have a feeling that the star of wonder will show me more about how to give love to the world. And what could be more adventurous than that?"

"Well, *she* was interesting!" said Sumar. "I hope we see her again sometime!"

"I have a feeling we will," said Princess Phoebe. "It's almost like she knew us already, like she already cared about us."

As they fed Jasmine the Camel, Sumar pointed out to Princess Phoebe that Jasmine's wounds, and their own, had healed almost completely. There was no explanation for such a rapid recovery, but they were both happy and grateful.

Many years later, when they thought about it, they realized that they'd learned to see miracles and wonders of all kinds, and some things just can't be explained.

"Now that Jasmine the Camel is healing so well, we should try to catch up to my brave brothers," Princess Phoebe said enthusiastically.

"But what if we leave this place and they come back and we're not here? Then we might not find them at all." Sumar sat down on a camel blanket and scratched his head, looking a little worried. *This is a most challenging moment*, he thought.

Princess Phoebe sat on another camel blanket, and thought so hard that her face scrunched. *This is a most challenging moment*, she thought.

What should they do?

What would *you* do?

How does one know what to do when one has never faced such a **most challenging moment** before?

Princess Phoebe looked at the bracelet on her arm, and thought about each of the beautiful beads. *What would Nana Anna say?* she wondered.

★ ★ ★

Princess Phoebe and Sumar listened to the wind and looked into the sky as the first stars of night began to twinkle. They listened to their own hearts and they listened to the Creator of Creation. And they both began to feel *peaceful* and *unafraid.*

"I feel peaceful right now," said Princess Phoebe, "but I don't know why."

"Me too," said Sumar, "and unafraid. No clue why, but that's okay."

Many years later, during another **very challenging moment**, they would listen to the wind and watch the evening stars and listen to their own hearts and to the Creator of Creation, because they never forgot **that night in the desert** when they learned what to do first in a **most challenging moment**.

The three princes rode their camels away from the baby king and into the great desert, being very careful to go a **long way around** so that Grumpy King Nefarious could not see them at all from his big fancy castle.

Late that evening, they stopped to rest at a small well surrounded by a few tall palm trees.

"This well must be so deep," said Prince Jonah, "because these trees are so tall."

Prince Nathan and Prince Jacob nodded, and both of them thought, *He is soooo smart.*

They took care of their camels, giving them water and food and a place to rest, because it's both good and wise to care for every animal and give them what they need.

Then they pulled their supplies from their camel bags.

"Uh-oh," said Prince Nathan. "The apricots are nearly gone."

"Uh-oh," said Prince Jacob. "Our crunchy nuts are almost gone too."

"Uh-oh," said Prince Jonah. "We have one small loaf of bread left. And it's kind of hard and all dried out."

"I'm not very hungry," said Prince Nathan, because his heart was full of love and kindness for his brothers. *But I'm a little hungry*, he thought.

"I'm not either," said Prince Jacob, because he wanted to play **kick-and-run** instead of eating.

"Me neither," said Prince Jonah, because he knew they might need to save their food until they were **really hungry.** *But I'm a little bit hungry*, he thought.

They decided to wait until they felt **very hungry**, and they started a little fire to keep themselves warm in the desert.

They drew some clear, cool water from the deep well, and drank until their thirst was all gone.

"This is such a fine well," said Nathan. "I wonder if other travelers stop here."

"I hope so! It would be fun to meet some new people!" Prince Jacob always liked to meet new people.

The three princely brothers sat quietly for a few minutes, and each one began to think about Royal Mama and Royal Papa and their home far away. *I feel a little bit ready for home*, each one thought.

I'm afraid we might be lost, thought Prince Jonah. *And I wonder if I'm wise enough to find our way home.*

I'm afraid we might run out of food and water,

thought Prince Nathan. *I wonder if I'm strong enough to keep going.*

I'm afraid we might run into lions or those nefarious guys, thought Prince Jacob. *And I wonder if I'm brave enough to face such dangers.*

Prince Jonah spoke softly. "I wonder what Mama and Papa are doing."

Prince Nathan whispered, "I miss them. Do you think they're angry with us for leaving without telling them?"

Prince Jacob said, "I hope they still love us."

The three brave princes felt sad together, and a **little bit afraid**. Everyone *has sad-and- afraid feelings*, but sometimes we can, indeed, feel sad and afraid together.

As the fire died down, the three brave and little-bit-sad-and-afraid princes fell asleep.

★ ★ ★

If you were to ride a camel for a day in the right direction, you would arrive atop a ginormous sand dune. And from the top of that dune, you would be able to see in every direction. And from that high point, you would be able see the three princes *and* the royal parents *and* the princess and Sumar. You would know that they were all near one another.

But alas, no one stood that day on the top of the ginormous dune, and so none of these fine people knew how close they were to each other. You, dear readers, are the only ones who know. What would you tell them to do?

★ ★ ★

CHAPTER 3

Princess Phoebe and Sumar had a **difficult talk** about what they should do. They disagreed. They both wanted to find the royal brothers, but Princess Phoebe now believed that staying put at their little oasis would be best.

"They know where we are, and they said they'd be back! If we leave and they come back, we may never see one another again!" She believed in her brothers and she loved them, and the thought of not seeing them again made her heart hurt.

"Yes, but Jasmine the Camel is all well, and can go fast! We can find them sooner if we leave here! We'll just go in the same direction that they went, and they'll be coming back that way, and we'll be together so much faster. Don't you want to see them sooner?" He put his hands on his hips and tilted his head sideways, a funny little habit of his that Princess Phoebe usually found amusing.

Princess Phoebe felt confused inside. Of course she wanted to see her brothers, and the sooner the better! She thought and thought, and she listened to her heart too, and then she knew.

She looked at Sumar and spoke. "Sumar, you are my best friend. It's hard for me to disagree with you. But this time I disagree with you. I know my brothers. No matter what happens, they will come here, right here, to be with us. So we must be here, right here, for that to happen."

She watched Sumar scratch his head, and then shrug. "I don't know if you are right. But I can see that you are certain. We will stay here."

Princess Phoebe and Sumar didn't talk much all day long. *It's hard and uncomfortable to disagree with someone you love*, they both thought.

That evening, Sumar and the princess made a small fire. When they opened the camel bags for something to eat, they found only two dried-up apricots and a handful of nuts.

I hope we've made the right decision, they both thought without saying it.

Princess Phoebe said, "I don't feel so hungry tonight."

Sumar said, "Me too."

"I wonder what our parents are eating tonight," Princess Phoebe said, thinking of the delicious food her mother and father made together.

"I wonder if our parents are very angry with us," Sumar said. "Maybe we should have talked to them about this adventure."

★ ★ ★

Less than a day's journey away, just beyond the second great sand dune in the eastern desert, the three worried grown-ups looked into the night sky.

Royal Mama spoke first. "When I see the moon and the stars, I remember that night when Princess Phoebe noticed the Great Star. She's so observant and smart. I'll bet she's watching the stars tonight, just like we are."

"And perhaps she and her royal brothers are following the star and following their dreams as we speak. I'm proud of them for their courage and curiosity. But I wish they'd talked to us before they left!"

Sumar's wise father spoke next. "Our children are brave, if not yet grown and wise in the ways of the world. Perhaps they will learn **important truths** in their adventures. Perhaps we will too."

"Yes, but I want to find them and hug them!" said Royal Mama. "Their adventure fills my heart with both **worry** and **love**."

The three worried grown-ups talked quietly that evening, and listened to the wind. And early the next morning, before the sun finished peeking over the horizon to begin the day, they set out toward the Great Star in the west.

★ ★ ★

And so, on the twelfth morning after their journey began, the three princes woke up a little bit hungry and a tiny bit homesick.

"I think we should be able to get to the oasis today, where Phoebe and Sumar are, if we leave early and try to go fast," said Prince Jonah.

"I'm already ready!" declared Prince Jacob, and indeed he was. He had already given his camel plenty of food and water, and he was eager to go.

"Not so fast!" called Prince Nathan, from the top of the nearby sand dune. "I think I see something—or someone—out on the desert!"

Jonah and Jacob scrambled up the dune as fast as they could, and shaded their eyes with their hands and looked *waaay* out into the desert.

A cloud of sandy dust, so far away that they could barely see it, seemed to be moving toward them.

"Who's that?" asked Jacob.

"Good question," said Jonah.

"Could be the bad guys," said Nathan. "Or maybe good guys."

"What should we do?" they all said at the same time.

⋆ ⋆ ⋆

What *should* they do? What if Grumpy King Nefarious sent his bad guys to hurt the princely brothers? On the other hand, what if Joseph and Mary and the baby king Jesus were trying to catch up with them? What if Princess Phoebe and Sumar decided to leave their oasis? Or, what if—the brothers didn't think of this, of course—but what if the sand blowing in the distance was the **three worried grown-ups**? Should the princely brothers wait to see who was coming? Or should they get away as fast as they could? What would *you* do, dear reader?

⋆ ⋆ ⋆

"We must think about this," said Prince Jonah. And they all sat down right there on top of the sand dune and thought very hard.

"Here's what I think," Prince Nathan said at last. "We don't know who that is, and we don't know what anyone else is doing. So I think we should do what we said we would do. We should return to the oasis where we left our sister and our friend. That's what we said we would do, so that is what we should do."

Prince Jonah and Prince Jacob agreed, and they all slid down the sand dune to prepare for their journey to the oasis.

I hope this is the right decision, they each thought without saying so. The princes were wise enough to know that sometimes doing the thing that seems right doesn't work out very smoothly after all.

In the middle of that day, when the sun was high and hot and the three princes were feeling tired and a **little concerned,** they stopped atop another sand dune and finally, finally, they could see the oasis far away in the distance!

"Yes!" they said, all together. And suddenly they didn't feel tired and hot any longer, and they knew they could be at the oasis before the sun went down.

They felt so happy and relieved!

But just as they begin riding down the dune on their camels, the faraway cloud of dust appeared, and it looked like it was headed for the oasis too.

"Oh no! Look at that!" cried Jacob. "What if that's the nefarious one? What if that's a bunch of bandits? What if that's a herd of wild mountain lions or elephants or desert snakes?" Prince Jacob had a remarkable imagination.

"We must hurry!" said Prince Nathan. "We have to get there before the bad guys, whoever they are!"

They galloped on their camels, and they galloped, and they galloped. The sun was so hot, and they were so thirsty, and the sand was so sandy as it flew into their eyes and ears and hair. But they galloped on, hoping and determined to get to the oasis before anyone could hurt their sister or their friend.

Their hearts pounded with fear and urgency and great love, as hearts were made to pound.

Far away across the desert, the three worried grown-ups noticed a cloud of dust and sand racing toward a small oasis in the distance.

"Someone's in a big hurry," said Royal Papa. "And it looks like they're headed to that little oasis."

"And that's exactly where I think our children must have stopped a few days ago!" said Sumar's very wise father. "We'd better hurry before whoever that is gets there!"

And so they raced on their camels, galloping as fast as the wind, with their hearts pounding with fear and urgency and enormous love, as hearts were made to pound.

★ ★ ★

Meanwhile, back at the old oasis, Princess Phoebe looked to the east.

"Oh my goodness!" she said. "Look at that cloud of dust and sand. It looks like it's headed straight this way!"

Sumar, looking in the opposite direction, said, "And look this way! Another cloud of dust and sand is moving toward us!"

"Maybe my brothers are coming!" Princess Phoebe jumped up and down. "Oh, I know it! My brothers are coming!"

Sumar looked a **little concerned**. "Maybe, but what if that cloud is not your brothers? And even if it is"—he pointed to the east—"who are *those* guys?"

"What should we do?" Princess Phoebe and Sumar said, at the exact same time. Indeed, what should they do? What would you tell them to do?

"We can't stay here," said Sumar. "Either one of those could be bad guys. Maybe both of them!"

"But we can't leave here," said Phoebe.

"Why not?" asked Sumar.

"Because Jasmine the Camel is missing!" said Phoebe.

And both of them felt **a little bit like crying**.

Jasmine the Camel was gone. Gone . . . gone . . . gone!

"How could she be gone?" Sumar shouted.

"Why would she go away?" Princess Phoebe shouted.

"Where could she be?" they shouted together.

They sat down on the camel blankets in the shade of the palm trees.

"This is the **worst day ever**," Princess Phoebe declared.

"Everything will be all right," said Sumar.

"No. It's not all right."

"But it will be all right. Someone is coming. I know it."

"Maybe. But that's not the problem!" Princess Phoebe held her hand up. "Look! Look, Sumar! My beautiful bracelet of colorful beads is gone! It must have broken in the night, or when I was digging in the sand, or— Oh, I don't know. But it's gone!"

"It's just a bracelet, Princess Phoebe. You don't have to have a bracelet to be all right." Sumar tried to say this **very gently** because he knew that the colorful bracelet was so special to Princess Phoebe.

Princess Phoebe gave Sumar her **most serious look**. "Of course I know that. That's not the point."

"Oh." Sumar knew this was not a good time to argue.

The clouds of dust and sand came a little closer. How far away were they? It was hard to tell.

Princess Phoebe and Sumar tried not to worry about Jasmine the Camel. And they tried not to worry about the **clouds of dust and sand** that were getting closer and closer.

Late in the afternoon, Princess Phoebe said, "I've been trying and trying not to worry. But I'm a little bit worried.'

"Me too," said Sumar. "I'm trying very hard not to be scared. But I'm a little bit scared."

"We'll stick together, no matter what," said Phoebe.

"Yes," agreed Sumar.

And both of their hearts pounded with fear and urgency and great love, as hearts were made to pound.

★ ★ ★

The sun began to fade away at the place where the earth and the sky meet, and the bright light of day grew dim, and it was getting hard to see the clouds of sand and dust. But they were definitely **getting very close.**

Princess Phoebe and Sumar sat on their blankets, back-to-back. Princess Phoebe looked to the east, and Sumar looked to the west. Soon it was too dark to see anything at all, and they looked up into the sky. The sliver of moon reminded Sumar of a melon slice. It reminded Princess Phoebe of a smile.

"*I see the moon, and the moon sees me, and the moon sees the one that I want to see,*" she sang.

"*God bless the moon and God bless me, and God bless the ones that I want to see,*" sang Sumar.

And then they were quiet.

And in the quiet they heard something.

"Do you hear that?" asked Sumar.

"Yes, what is that? It almost sounds like faraway thunder, but there's no storm."

The thundering noise grew louder

and LOUDER

and LOUDER!

"It's coming from that way!" Sumar shouted, pointing west.

"No, it's coming from that way!" Princess Phoebe pointed east.

And then, suddenly, they were in the midst of a big cloud of sand and dust and couldn't see anything at all!

A man's voice came from the dust. "Sumar! Sumar, are you here?"

"Papa!" Sumar shouted.

A princely voice called out, "Princess Phoebe, are you here?"

"Jonah!" Phoebe shouted.

"My children!" a voice called out.

"Mama!" the four royal children shouted.

★ ★ ★

"How did you find us?" Prince Jonah asked the grown-ups.

"Well, at first we thought perhaps you'd gone to the shore to play, but we didn't find you there," said Royal Papa. "And then we thought perhaps you'd gone to the Big Village, but we didn't find you there. And then we remembered how curious you all were about the Great Shining Star, and we said, 'Aha! They're full of wonder and they've gone to follow the star!'"

"We did! We followed the star!" said Jacob.

"And we fought lions!" said Phoebe.

And just then, Nana Anna galloped right up to the oasis on that silly Jasmine the Camel! "Look who I found!" she called out happily!

"And we met this sweet lady!" said Sumar. And they all hugged and hugged.

"And we ate in the palace of the grumpy nefarious king!" said Prince Nathan.

"And we saw the baby king Jesus! And he smiled on us with **perfect love**!" reported Prince Jacob.

"But we lost Jasmine the Camel," said Sumar.

"And I lost the beautiful bracelet Nana Anna gave me," said Princess Phoebe.

"And we got a **little bit lost**," said Prince Jonah.

The grown-ups opened their camel bags and brought out juicy grapes and fresh bread and delicious cheeses and sweet figs and cool water, and they all sat on the blankets telling their stories of adventure and fear and love.

Prince Jacob wiggled his toes in the cool sand and felt something. He picked it up—a shining red bead. "What's this?" he asked, holding it up in the starlight.

"Why, that's the red bead from my bracelet!" said Princess Phoebe. "It's to remind you that whenever you're angry or hurt, you're not alone, and that you have enough strength inside of you and enough love around you to get through the hard and scary moments in life. Oh, brother Jacob, that's perfect for you! You must keep that bead forever!"

"Look, I found one too!" said Nathan, holding up a brilliant blue bead.

Princess Phoebe explained, "It's blue like the sky and the water, a reminder of perfect and true **love**, surrounding us always. That's perfect for you, brother Nathan!"

"And here's a green one!" cried Prince Jonah.

"Oh," said Phoebe, "that is so you, brother Jonah! It's the color of life—trees and growing things—to remind you that life is a good and wondrous gift, to cherish and celebrate!"

"And this one is golden!" Sumar smiled.

"Indeed, it is pure gold! It's to remind you that the sun comes up every day, no matter what, and that every new day is an invitation to open your heart to love and goodness. Sumar, you have shown us that kind of love throughout your friendship. You must keep the golden bead!"

"What about this bead?" asked Royal Mama, smiling and holding the very pink bead. "This must be yours, Princess Phoebe, because it shines with joy!"

Princess Phoebe held the perfectly pink bead in her hands. "Yes," she said, "joy, no matter what, because **life** is grand and **love** is real and **beauty** is everywhere!"

"I saw that in our journey together," said Prince Jonah.

"I saw it in our care for each other," said Prince Nathan.

"I saw it in the face of the baby king Jesus," said Prince Jacob.

"I see it now in our parents' love and our friendship," said Sumar.

"I see it everywhere I look!" said Phoebe, pointing toward the sky and smiling at Nana Anna.

They all looked up and their fears disappeared, and the night sky began to sparkle!

Stars began to dance and shoot across the sky!

The brave princess and three brave princes and Sumar and the parents and Nana Anna all looked up into the sky, and there they watched a stunning, shining, sparkling spectacle of light—dazzling, dancing light, glimmering and glowing. It looked like angels dancing in the sky.

Many centuries later, people sometimes witnessed what they would call a **meteor shower**, but that's only a little bit like the bright, brilliant, beautiful light of pure love that appeared that night in the desert sky.

Prince Jacob sang, "*Star of Wonder, star of night, star with royal beauty bright, westward leading, still proceeding, guide us with thy perfect light.*"

They all sang it together, their voices and hearts full of **wonder**.

And the **perfect light**, the very light of **perfect love**,
fell on each of them and shone through them,
and they hugged one another,
and their hearts beat gladly
with **wonder** and **gratitude** and **joy** and **great love**,
as all our hearts are meant and made to beat.

•ABOUT THE AUTHOR•

Rebecca Dwight Bruff is the author of the award-winning debut novel, *Trouble the Water*, published June 2019, and the non-fiction book, *Loving the World with God*, published 2014. Bruff earned her Bachelors degree in education at Texas A&M University and Master and Doctorate degrees in theology, both from Southern Methodist University. In 2017, she was a scholarship recipient for the prestigious Key West Literary Seminar. She volunteers at the Pat Conroy Literary Center in Beaufort, South Carolina. She's published non-fiction, plays a little tennis, travels when she can, and loves life in the lowcountry with her husband and an exuberant golden retriever. www.rebeccabruff.com

•ABOUT THE ILLUSTRATOR•

Jill Dubin's whimsical art has appeared in over 40 children's books, including *Over on a Mountain, Seeds Grow,* and *I Can Cooperate!* She graduated from Pratt Institute and currently lives with her family in Cape Cod, Massachusetts. www.jilldubin.com

CPSIA information can be obtained
at www.ICGtesting.com
Printed in the USA
JSHW040522180920
7994JS00004B/68